NEVER
TALK TO STRANGERS

ISBN 0-439-21689-3

12 11 10 9 8 7 6 5 4 3 2 1   2 3 4 5/0

Printed in the U.S.A.   24

First Scholastic printing, September 2000

NEVER
TALK TO STRANGERS

by irma joyce illustrated by s.d. schindler

SCHOLASTIC INC.

New York Toronto London Auckland Sydney
Mexico City New Delhi Hong Kong

If you are hanging from a trapeze
And up sneaks a camel with bony knees,
Remember this rule, if you please—
Never talk to strangers.

If you are shopping in a store
And a spotted leopard leaps through the door,
Don't ask him what he's shopping for.
Never talk to strangers.

If the doorbell rings and standing there
Is a grouchy, grumbling grizzly bear,
Don't open the door. Mom won't care.
Never talk to strangers.

If you are waiting for a bus
And behind you stands a rhinoceros,
Though he may shove and make a fuss,
Never talk to strangers.

If you are out for a mountain climb
And a coyote asks if you know the time,
Let him wait for a clock to chime.
Never talk to strangers.

If you are mailing a letter to Aunt Lucille
And you see a car with a whale at the wheel,
Stay away from him and his automobile.
Never talk to strangers.

If you are riding your bike at noon
And you see a bee with a bass bassoon,
Don't stop to ask the name of his tune.
Never talk to strangers.

If you are swimming in a pool
And a crocodile begins to drool,
Paddle away and repeat this rule—
Never talk to strangers.

But . . . if your father introduces you
To a roly-poly kangaroo,
Say politely, "How do you do?"
Because your family knows her.

If a pal of yours you've always known
Brings around a prancing roan,
Welcome him in a friendly tone.
Because your old pal knows him.

If while eating toast and honey,
You catch a glimpse of the Easter Bunny,
Tell him a joke. He'll think it's funny.
And . . . everybody knows him.

Now I'll tell you why you've never heard
This jolly giraffe say a single word.
It's because she learned from a little bird—
Never talk to strangers!